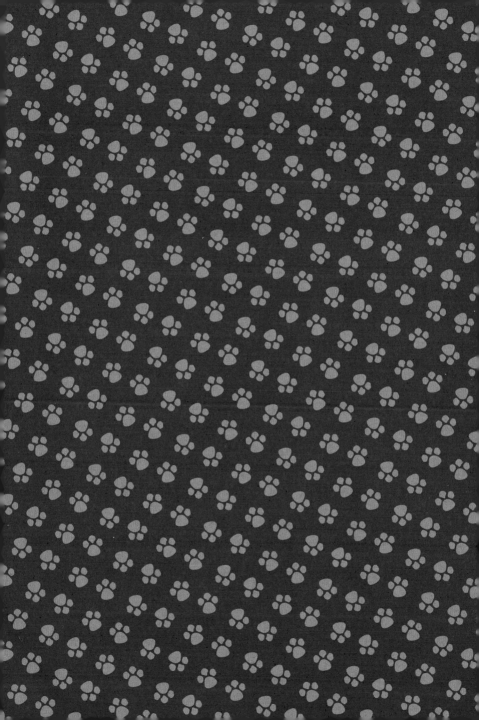

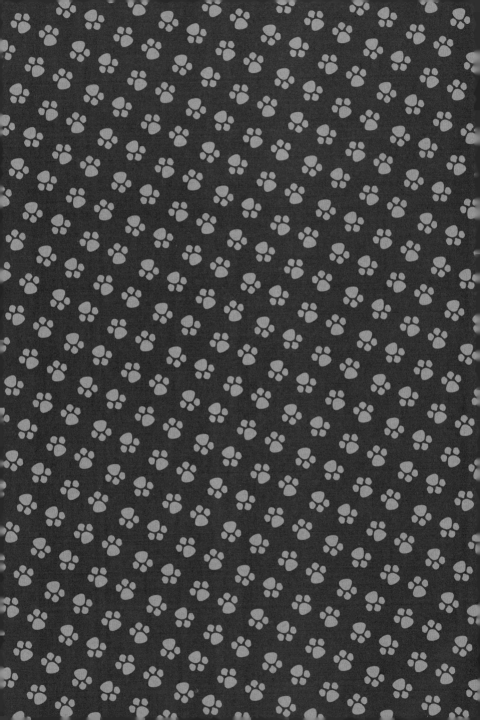

HELPER HOUNDS

Noodle

Helps Gabriel Say Goodbye

Dedication
To Jennifer Grant
Thanks for introducing me to Gus, Noodle's inspiration-dog, for cheering me on in my writing, and for believing in animal rescue as much as I do.

To Chicago's Anti-Cruelty Society
This is where I imagined Noodle. Grateful for the good work you all do.

HELPER HOUNDS

Noodle

Helps Gabriel Say Goodbye

Caryn Rivadeneira

Illustrated by Priscilla Alpaugh

RED CHAIR PRESS

Egremont, Massachusetts

RED CHAIR PRESS
BOOKS FOR YOUNG READERS

www.redchairpress.com

Publisher's Cataloging-In-Publication Data

Names: Rivadeneira, Caryn Dahlstrand, author | Alpaugh, Priscilla, illustrator.

Title: Noodle helps Gabriel say goodbye / Caryn Rivadeneira ; illustrated by Priscilla Alpaugh.

Description: Egremont, Massachusetts : Red Chair Press, [2020] | Series: Helper hounds | Summary: "After losing her first two forever homes, Noodle knows all about the sadness of goodbyes. But in her new home with Andrea and as an official Helper Hound, Noodle helps Gabriel deal with the loss of his grandfather"-- Provided by publisher.

Identifiers: ISBN 9781634409155 (library hardcover) | ISBN 9781634409186 (paperback) | ISBN 9781634409216 (ebook)

Subjects: LCSH: Dogs--Juvenile fiction. | Human-animal relationships--Juvenile fiction. | Loss (Psychology)--Juvenile fiction. | Grandfathers--Death--Psychological aspects--Juvenile fiction. |CYAC: Dogs--Fiction. | Human-animal relationships--Fiction. | Loss (Psychology)--Fiction. | Grandfathers--Death--Psychological aspects--Fiction.

Classification: LCC PZ7.1.R57627 No 2020 | DDC [E]--dc23

Library of Congress Control Number: 2019951548

Photos: iStock

Printed in the United States of America

0520 1P CGF20

CHAPTER 1

My nose worked through the weeds,
wildflowers, and tall grasses along the fence.
Of all my favorite spots on the campus of
North Branch University—the wide lawn, the
cafeteria dumpsters, the porch on Old Main,
the beanbags outside the library, the welcome
fountain, the alley behind our house—this path
along the river is my favorite. After all, this is
the place where I could play my favorite game:
Guess That Animal Smell.

It's a simple game. Try it sometime. Rules go
like this:

Sniff the dirt, a bush, a tree, a stump, or the

fence. Then you match the smell with the ugly mugs of all the animals you know. Then you guess.

Sniff, sniff.
Match, match. Guess, guess.

Badger! No, raccoon! Wait… Otter? Could it be? Yes, otter!

Since it's a game you play by yourself, you decide who wins. And guess what? I always win! I'm great at sniffing out the creatures that live along the river that runs through campus — and the city that we're in.

But, I also love this spot because of the trees and tree stumps that line the river. The students come here to wander through the trees and to sit on the stumps and "chill out," as Andrea calls it. She says they need to breathe some woodland air in the middle of the city as they experience nature and relax.

That may be, but when I bump into the students (which is every time I'm out here), I know they come here to see me. Because every time they see me, the students smile and shout my name: "Noodle!" And though they talk to Andrea, they kneel down and scrub their fingers into my hair and tell me all their troubles, worries, hopes, and about how much they miss their dogs back home.

I listen to them. They pet me. It's a win-win!

And today proved to be no different.

"Noodle!"

I jerked my head up from the base of the pine tree I was sniffing. I was this-close to guessing squirrel (Stubby the Squirrel to be exact). But that would have to wait. A student was calling me. I looked toward the voice.

Nate! He was one of the best students here at North Branch University.

I strained at the end of my leash to get to him further up the path.

"Easy, Noodle," Andrea said.

I slowed down—at least, until Nate said my name again. This time Nathan said it *nice and slowly* like I liked it. In fact, Nathan kept the *Noooooooooddddllllle* going as he knelt down with lips stuck out in a kiss to greet me. I loved that.

"Hey Nate," Andrea said. "A little chilly out here today, huh?"

"Nah," Nate said. "Feels good. Soccer practice was rough. Coach Colbert ran us hard."

"Well, you have a big match on Saturday," Andrea said. "Folks coming?"

"Nah," he said. "Dad's not doing great. Mom is worried about driving too far from his doctors."

"I'm sorry to hear that," Andrea said. "Tell your folks I said hello. And how about you drop by the house sometime next week for dinner? Ann would love to hear about this season's team."

Nate smiled and nodded. Then he dug his

fingers deeper into my curly hair and said, "Noodle, you make me miss my girl. I wish you could meet her."

Nate had told me all about his dog, Toast. Toast was an *actual* poodle, Nate said. Not like me. I'm a Doodle—a standard poodle mixed with a Golden Retriever. Last time we talked, Nate wondered why anyone would mix up an actual poodle. He said they were the smartest, most athletic, best dogs around. "Why mess with perfection?" he asked.

Andrea said something about how she didn't like it either. But, she didn't like *anyone* breeding dogs for any reason.

"Rescued is the best breed!" Andrea always said.

I was sure glad Andrea rescued me—actual poodle or not!

"Any Helper Hounds cases coming up?" Nate asked.

"In fact," Andrea said. "We need to get back to the house. I just got a text about a boy having trouble getting over feeling angry that his grandfather died. He doesn't let himself cry and won't go visit the cemetery."

Nate sighed and looked toward the ground.

"I don't blame the kid for being angry," Nate said. "I'm angry about my dad being so sick too. I don't want him to die."

Andrea put her arm on Nate's.

"Your dad is going to be okay," she said. "I just know it."

Nate nodded. "That's what the doctors say. But I worry, you know?"

"I do know," Andrea said. "And any time you need to talk or hang out with Noodle, stop by, okay? Petting Noodle helps a lot with worry."

"It does," Nate said. "She'll be able to help that boy with his grief too. She knows a thing or two about that right?"

Andrea smiled.

"Yup," Andrea said as she reached down to scratch me. "Noodle knows all about grief. She's had to grieve two families now. Poor fuzzy girl."

Andrea reached down to scratch the fluff on the top of my head.

"Yeah," Nate said. "That's the tree you planted in honor of her old man, right?"

Andrea looked over to the small maple tree growing between the giant elms and pines.

"That's the one!" Andrea said. "Curly keeps peeing on the plaque. I think that's how she honors his memory!"

Nate laughed.

"Yeah, maybe," he said. "But she's been through so much and keeps on loving whoever she meets. She's a great role model. Maybe not the part about peeing."

Andrea and Nate laughed. A clock chime rang in the distance.

"Shoot," Nate said. "It's seven. Better get back to my homework. Thanks for chatting. Bye, Andrea. Bye, Noodle."

"Let me know about dinner," Andrea said.

Nate nodded and pet me one more time. My tail swished and swished. As we watched Nate walk away, I smelled the smallest bit of skunk rising from the riverbanks.

I pulled toward the river, but Andrea changed direction.

"You heard me," she laughed. "Gotta get back and see how we can help Gabriel. We need to help him with his anger and his grief."

I could do that. I may not be an *actual* full-blood poodle, but I am an actual Helper Hound. But that wasn't the only reason. Andrea was right. I've loved—and lost—two families now. I know how sad and scary that is. Before we get to Gabriel, let me tell you my story.

CHAPTER 2

The dogs in the kennels around me barked.
I lifted my head off my cot. I heard a man
shuffling on the cement outside our gates. I
stretched and put my paws down on the cool
kennel floor and took two quick sniffs to get
more information.

Lemon. Honey. It smelled like the drink my
boy's mom used to bring him before bedtime to
help him sleep when he got his coughs.

Poor Jimmy. He had trouble breathing, and
he really wanted a dog. Jimmy's doctor said not
to get him one because of Jimmy's allergies. But
his mom and dad said every boy deserved a

dog—allergic or not. So Jimmy's parents plunked out two thousand dollars to get me from a "good breeder" because I was "hypo-allergenic." That meant, because I have *hair* and not *fur*, I'm not supposed to make people cough and sneeze. Turns out, it's not always true. (Andrea says a "good breeder" should know this and not sell dogs to people with terrible allergies.)

But, whenever Jimmy and I played together (which was a lot), he coughed and wheezed. Jimmy cried when his mom said I would have to go. I hoped his tears would change his mom's mind, but it didn't. She said they would have to try another kind of dog because I didn't work out for him.

I thought I was working just fine. But one day, when Jimmy was at school, his mom brought me to the animal shelter. I didn't even get a chance to say goodbye to Jimmy. That was really sad.

But the people at the shelter were very nice. They fed me, walked me, gave me a stuffed monkey to play with, and loved me when they could. But it got lonely there. I missed playing with Jimmy. At night I would lie in my little cot and wonder if Jimmy was playing with another dog—and if he loved that dog like he loved me. I wondered if I'd ever get to play with another boy—and if I'd love that boy as much as I loved Jimmy. I couldn't imagine it. Jimmy was the best.

During the day, I learned to scoot toward the front of my kennel when people approached. If the people looked nice (and they almost always did), I would bark once—maybe twice—to get attention and then sit with my tongue out. Sometimes I'd tilt my head. The nice people would stop and admire my shaggy red curls or my huge head. I'd stand, wag my tail, and let my tongue droop further. Then, almost always, once of the nice people would say, "She's adorable. She's just *so big.*" And then they would move on to the other dogs.

The thing is, I was just a little puppy when Jimmy's family got me. But now, I am big, and my fluffy hair makes me look even bigger—especially my head.

One day, Kelly at the shelter said I should get "shorn" like her sheep.

"You'll look smaller," she says. "But you'll also look less curly!"

Since my name was Curly back then, I guess it was important that I looked curly. So they decided to keep my hair big and curly. Turned out, being curly didn't matter so much. My name was about to change—sort of.

CHAPTER 3

The man squinted at the card on my kennel gate. I sniffed and sniffed his honey-and-lemon smell. He reached into his pocket and pulled out a pair of glasses.

"Curly?" the man said. "The Golden Doodle?"

I sat and let my tail swish on the cement floor.

"Curly the Doodle doesn't work at all," he said.

My head drooped. This was the second time someone told me I didn't work.

"No," the man removed his glasses and looked straight at me. "You're a Curly Noodle the Doodle if I ever saw one."

Then he leaned on his cane and bent closer to me. The man reached a finger through the fence and scratched my head.

"This mop you've got is like a bowl of macaroni," he said. "Like my wife used to make. Do you like macaroni?"

My mind drifted back to the bright orange noodles that Jimmy used to slip me under the table. A small puddle of drool formed by my feet.

"I could make us some, I suppose, if you do like macaroni," the man said.

I liked where this was going.

"Excuse me," the man said.

Kelly stopped in front of my kennel.

"Yes?" Kelly said as she waved to me. "Hi, Curly!"

"Could you tell me about this dog?"

"I'd love to," Kelly said. And she told the man all about Jimmy and his coughing and how much I loved to play fetch and roll around.

"Well," the man said. "I don't have much wrestle left in me. But I live near a college. I could walk her there every day and she'd have no shortage of young people to play with—if she missed that."

"How about you and I go talk for a moment and then we can see if you two can't get to know one another?" Kelly asked.

The man nodded and reached a finger

through the gate to pet me.

"See you soon, Noodle," the man said.

I watched him walk away.

• • •

I slurped my water in the corner.

"Curly—er, Noodle."

I looked up.

Kelly stood in front of my kennel with a leash in her hands. I loved this part of the day! A walk!

But this wouldn't be a regular walk. The man stood next to Kelly.

I jumped and jumped and acted all kinds of wild while Kelly tried to connect my leash to my collar.

"Curly," Kelly said. "Mind your manners. Sit please."

I sat.

Kelly clipped my leash on. I left the kennel

like a bolt of lightning.

Kelly pulled back on the leash and called my name. The man watched, his eyes wide.

"She calms down when she gets outside," Kelly said. "I promise."

And she was right. I always wanted to run past the kennels. Every time a dog walked past the other dogs, every dog in the place barked and barked and barked. It got stressful—so I walked fast! Besides, I had to pee and I wanted to be *outside!*

But once I was outside—and able to hear the neighborhood sounds of trucks and birds and kids running in the playground across the street—I settled right down.

After I peed, Kelly handed the man my leash.

I'd never walked with someone who used a cane before. I sniffed it as the man took my leash.

"Not all dogs are crazy about canes," Kelly said. "It makes some dogs nervous. Curly just seems interested. That's good."

We walked around the parking lot and through the small patch of grass and trees. I sniffed and sniffed. That skunk had been here recently, ten, maybe twelve, hours ago. I put my nose to the wind. Which way did it go…

Before I could figure that out, Kelly called us toward the picnic tables. The man and Kelly sat. Kelly told me to go sit. So I sat—and decided to rest my chin on the man's knee. It seemed like he could use that. I did too.

"She's a good girl," the man said as he scratched my head. "She walks like a dream. Is it a problem that I live in an apartment?"

"Normally we prefer bigger energetic dogs like Curly to be in spaces where they can run around," Kelly said. "But you said you take daily walks through the college campus?"

"My morning, noon, and evening ritual," the man said. "My wife and I took those walks for

30 years together. I haven't missed a day since she died. It's nice to stop and talk to the kids, but I miss walking *with* someone."

Kelly smiled and leaned down to kiss me. I kissed her back.

"Whatcha think, Curly? Do all those walks sound like fun? Would you like to go home with Mr. Fusilli?"

I stood up, hoping they'd understand that I was ready to go.

Mr. Fusilli reached for his cane, but it tipped over before he could grab it. I've picked up lots of sticks in my life. So I just picked up that one for him too. Kelly and Mr. Fusilli thought that was great. They both laughed until Kelly stopped and said: "Wait a minute. *Fusilli.* Isn't that a kind of curly pasta?"

"It is!" Mr. Fusilli said. "It's a curly noodle. That's how I knew this was the dog for me."

CHAPTER 4

So that's how I came to live with Mr. Fusilli. I
lived in his apartment for two of the best years.
Just like he told Kelly at the shelter, every single
day—rain, shine, sun, or snow—we walked
through the college campus near
our apartment. It was the
best. I loved the smells
and the students.

The students would
see me and come
running. They were
all happy to sink
their hands into my

hair and scratch my back or to squat down and tell me about their days. Sometimes they'd sneak me a treat, something left over from their cafeteria.

When we'd get back, Mr. Fusilli would read his paper on the sofa in the sunroom and sip his honey-and-lemon tea. I'd stretch out next to him and catch a snooze or two.

Sometimes I still thought about Jimmy. I wished I could see him. But my life with Mr. Fusilli was good. I loved Mr. Fusilli, and he loved me.

Then one day, Mr. Fusilli didn't get up. I put my head on his chest to remind him that it was time for our "morning ritual," but he didn't move. I knew something was wrong. So I climbed on the bed and curled up next to Mr. Fusilli to see if that would help.

I watched the sun rise again and again from the bed.

I whimpered and barked, but no one heard me. It got pretty lonely in the apartment—and I felt bad for peeing and pooping under the dining room table. I felt even worse for jumping on the counter and grabbing the loaf of bread and ripping open a bag of chips. But I was hungry—and I had to go!

Then one day, I heard a loud knock on the door.

"Mr. Fusilli?" a voice said. "Chicago Police. Everything okay in there?"

"Mr. Fusilli?" another voice said. "It's Andrea. From North Branch University. Are you in there?"

I ran to the door and barked. And barked and barked and barked.

The door opened hard and hit me in the head.

"Oh, baby," Andrea said as she rubbed my head. "Are you okay?"

But I didn't have time for that. I ran back to

Mr. Fusilli's room. Andrea and the police officer followed me. The police officer looked in the room first. He shrugged his shoulder and spoke into the radio on his shirt.

Andrea started crying and knelt down to hug me.

"Oh, no," she said. "I'm so sorry. Some of the kids at the college were worried about you. They said they hadn't seen you and Mr. Fusilli for a few days. I wish I noticed sooner."

Pretty soon, the apartment was filled with firefighters and paramedics. They let me sniff Mr. Fusilli goodbye before they wheeled him out on a gurney.

It was sad.

"Seems he doesn't have any family. I'll call animal control," the police officer said to Andrea. "They'll take Noodle to the pound. Shame. She's a sweet dog."

Andrea caught her breath and shook her head.

"No," she said. "Noodle loves being on campus. She belongs there. If it's okay, I'll take her home."

The officer handed Andrea my leash and his card.

"If you change your mind, call me."

Andrea thanked the officer and wiped her tears.

"Well, Noodle," Andrea said. "Mr. Fusilli told me the story of how you came to live with him and how well you adjusted to your new life. Are you ready for another new life with me and Ann?"

I hadn't been ready for a life without Jimmy and I wasn't ready for life without Mr. Fusilli. But I knew one thing: we can lose people we love but somehow there are always more people to love.

So I went to live with Andrea and Ann in the big house on the North Branch campus. I loved Andrea and Ann, the walks, and all my students. I settled in to my daily routine of walking through campus and sometimes hanging out with students in the library or entertaining guests when Ann and Andrea held big parties for donors or famous alumni. I was always a big hit.

One night, a man named Mr. Tuttle showed up at one of these parties. He was the founder of Helper Hounds. Years ago, the Helper Hounds had come to campus to help students after a bomb scare on campus, and Mr. Tuttle was back to guest-lecture in a class.

Long story short: Andrea told Mr. Tuttle how I loved to sit with students in the library and listen as they told me their problems while on walks. She told him how I had lived with a boy, and then with Mr. Fusilli, and how I came to North Branch University. Mr. Tuttle listened hard and then asked me to do a few tricks.

I sat. I lay down. I came when he called. I let him lift up my paws and look at my teeth. I really do have good teeth.

Mr. Tuttle then asked the question that would change my whole life: "Would you like to bring Noodle to Helper Hounds University? See how she does?"

Andrea tilted her head and looked at me. "Curly Noodle? A Helper Hound?"

I tilted my head back at both of them and barked.

"Sounds like she wants to give it a go," Mr. Tuttle said.

And so we did. After many weeks of classes and tests and meeting lots of other dogs and people, I got my very own red Helper Hounds badge and vest. I've been a world-famous Helper Hound for two years now. We go all around the world helping people with all sorts of things.

Every day I still miss Jimmy and Mr. Fusilli. But helping people is what I was born to do. Which reminds me: we better get back to Gabriel's story!

CHAPTER 5

Most of the time, when we get a new Helper Hounds case, Andrea and I travel far away. Usually we hop in the car and drive a couple hours. Sometimes we even get on an airplane! But Gabriel lived just a few blocks from campus. So Andrea slipped on my vest, snapped on my leash, and off we walked. We cut through campus, taking the bridge across the river to the street filled with townhouses, apartment buildings, and three-flats just down the way from us.

As we passed the trees and river, I caught whiffs of the familiar squirrels, skunks, possums, raccoons, and otters. But when I'm wearing my vest, we don't stop to sniff. I'm on duty. I'm at work. So I was fully focused ahead when I spotted a boy in the middle of the sidewalk ahead of me.

The boy pointed at me and ran back toward his apartment building.

"Mama," he yelled. "*La perra esta aqui! La perra esta aqui!*"

A woman in an apron that smelled like beef stew stepped out from the building.

"Ay," the woman said. "*Que linda.*"

Andrea told me to sit and she stuck out her hand when we reached the walkway in front of Gabriel's building.

"I'm Andrea," she said. "I'm sorry I don't speak much Spanish."

"It's okay," the woman said. "I'm Rosita, Gabriel's *abuela*. You can call me *Abuela*, if you want. Everyone else does. Gabriel! Come back outside!"

"And this," Andrea said, "is Noodle."

"She's beautiful," Rosita said. "But I still don't understand how a dog helps a child understand death?"

At this, Rosita made the sign of a cross on her body and clenched beads that draped her hands.

"Good question," Andrea said. "The Helper Hounds 'teach' by being there for comfort. Kids tend to talk more around the dogs than they do people. That's what we hope for. That's how Noodle can help."

"Gabriel needs to talk, poor boy," Abuela said. "He was so broken up when my husband died. So sad. And yet, he does not cry. He just gets angry that his grandfather is gone."

Rosita quickly wiped a tear and smiled as a woman walked up with Gabriel.

"Isabel," Abeula said. "This is Andrea and Noodle."

They shook hands.

"We're so happy you're here," Isabel said. "Do you really live on North Branch's campus? So close? I went to school there, you know."

"You did? Fantastic!" Andrea said. "And yes, we really do live there. My partner's the university president. We've been there eight years now. I've had Noodle for four of those years."

Isabel knelt down and made kissing sounds in front of my face.

"I'm so happy you're here," she said. I gave her two slurps on the lips since she asked so nicely. "Gabriel, *mi amor*, say hello to Noodle."

Gabriel walked up and stuck out his hand.

"Not sure she can shake your hand, *niño*," his mother said.

But I knew this drill all too well. I lifted my paw and set it in Gabriel's hand. He shook it.

"She's smart!" Gabriel said.

"She is," Andrea said. "Noodle's also very

well trained. And she's learned what people want—and need—and is happy to help."

"My mom wants her to help me not feel mad about my abuelo dying," Gabriel said. "She's supposed to help me cry or something."

Gabriel rolled his eyes at his mom.

"You and your sassy mouth," Abuela said and she swatted the bottom of her apron at

Gabriel. The smell of stew wafted toward me. I was mid-drool when Andrea said: "How about you walk Noodle inside for me and we can all talk about how Noodle can help? But I promise: she's not here to make you cry."

"Good," Gabriel said. "I hate crying."

"Me too," Andrea whispered as she handed Gabriel her leash.

"But Noodle has lost people too," Andrea said. "Her first boy was allergic to her. So they had to give her away. Her second boy—a grown-up grandpa—died. You two might have things to talk about."

Gabriel shrugged.

"I guess," he said. "But do I really get to walk her?" His face lit up.

"Sure do," Andrea said. "Lead the way."

Gabriel walked me up a sidewalk and through a door. "We're on the third floor," Gabriel said. "Wanna race me?"

"She won't race while she's in her vest,"
Andrea said. "Hold on."

Andrea reached down and unclipped my
vest. I shook all my curly noodles out and took
off up the stairs as Gabriel skipped two at a
time. I'd never been in this building before—
but the stairs were just like some of the dorms
at school. Each staircase led to a small landing
with a window and a quick turn and then
another set of stairs. I beat Gabriel up the
stairs—but it was close.

Andrea, Isabel, and Abuela were not even
to the first landing, but Andrea's voice came
through loud and clear: "Sit," she said. "Stay."

I sat and stayed.

"Can I walk her into the apartment?" Gabriel
asked.

"She needs to wait for me and the vest,"
Andrea said. "We'll be there in a sec."

While we waited for everyone else, I stuck

my nose in the air and took two sniffs.

"That's cigar you smell," Gabriel said. "My abuelo smoked one every night on the fire escape. Abuela hated it. She said it was bad for his health and made the apartment stink. But I liked the smell. I'm glad we can still smell it."

Andrea, Isabel, and Abuela reached the top landing.

"I'm glad we can still smell it too, *mi amor*," Abuela said. She gave Gabriel a hug. He shirked away.

"I can't smell it without thinking of papi," Isabel said.

"Smelling cigar is a better way to remember than visiting dumb old graveyards," Gabriel said.

"*Ay me madre*," Abuela said. She looked toward the ceiling and crossed herself again.

Isabel shook her head, turned the door handle, and led us into Gabriel's apartment.

CHAPTER 6

Gabriel and I sat on the braided rug in the sunroom. The adults talked at a table in the dining room.

"They're whispering about me," Gabriel said while he tugged on the rope that dangled from my mouth. "They want me to go back to that cemetery to visit. Abuela says it's important to remember. But that place was so spooky. I can't stand to think of Abuelo in that box, all alone in a graveyard. I'm never going back."

Then Gabriel turned toward the table in the other room and said louder: "I'm *never* going back."

"Ay," said Gabriel's mom. "Now you understand our worry. He got pretty scared at the funeral."

"I'm not scared," Gabriel said.

Isabel shook her head.

"He and his abuelo were so close," she said. "His abuelo picked him up after school every day, they watched baseball together, they fed the ducks in the river... which I know we're not supposed to."

Andrea and Gabriel's mom laughed. Signs were posted all over campus and along the riverbanks about the dangers of feeding ducks. Everyone ignored them. (I wondered if people would obey them if the sign *also* instructed people instead to toss their cut-up chunks of bread to a certain curly-noodle of a dog…)

"So you're not *scared* about going to the cemetery," Andrea asked. "Why don't you want to go?"

"I'm mad he's there," Gabriel said. "That place is spooky."

"So maybe you're a little bit scared," Andrea said with a smile.

Gabriel shrugged.

"Can I tell you what used to scare me— when I was a girl?" Andrea said. "We can see if they match."

Gabriel nodded. He released the rope and sunk his fingers into the curls on my back.

"My mother died when I was seven—really young," Andrea said.

"*Que triste,*" Abuela said. "How sad."

"Yes," Andrea said. "It was. But I felt really angry too. My dad used to take us to the cemetery so we could 'talk' to our mom. But I hated it. I didn't want to think of her as dead or buried underground. I wanted to think of her as alive—and that she would come back home some day."

Gabriel nodded.

"That's why I like his cigar smell," Gabriel said. "I smell it and pretend he just went down to the corner to get a coffee and that he'll be right back."

Gabriel sniffed and leaned his head toward mine.

"I want Abuelo to come right back," Gabriel said. "If I go to the cemetery, I remember he won't be back. That he's dead. Forever. That makes me mad. The cemetery just proves that I'll never see him again."

"Niño," Abuela said. "I miss him too. He was my husband for forty years! But remember what Father Nuñez said at mass: we *will* see your abuelo again someday. It's what our faith teaches. We visit the cemetery to remember that one day we will all be together again."

Gabriel turned his head toward me and rolled his eyes.

"Who knows if that's true," Gabriel said. Abuela crossed herself and kissed the cross around her neck.

"Besides, I want him here now," Gabriel said. "Not later."

Gabriel took deep breaths and ran his hand down my back. I rested my head on his lap. I could smell the tears behind Gabriel's eyes. He was close to crying—but Gabriel sniffed and blinked and the tears went away.

"I still want my mom with me," Andrea said. "I wish she could be here now. That feeling doesn't go away. But you know what gets easier?"

Gabriel shook his head.

"Going to the cemetery, visiting places you used to go with them, and learning to see 'signs' of their presence in your life," she said.

"What does that mean?" Gabriel said.

"It means, that it took a while, but once I accepted that my mom really was dead, that she really was buried in that terrible cemetery, that she wasn't going to come back, I was able to 'see' her in new ways," Andrea said. "And with that, I started feeling less angry. I was still sad. Just not mad. In fact, I started to like going to the cemetery. I started talking to her there. But I also started talking to her in other places. I kept a journal and I'd write her letters every night. That way, she never seemed too far away.

And—are you ready for the weirdest part?"

Gabriel's mom and abuela leaned in. Gabriel's eyes grew wide and he nodded.

"Okay," Andrea said. "Once I stopped feeling so mad that she wasn't with me any more, I began to realize she wasn't far away after all. My mom made me who I am. She's part of me! Just like your abuelo made you who you are—and who your mom is, who Abuela is. That means, your abuelo is still part of you and your family."

Gabriel tilted his head. "I have no idea what you're talking about," he said.

Andrea nodded. "Okay," she said. "Take Noodle. She's got *hair*, not fur. That means she doesn't shed. Well, not really. But I

promise you, when we leave here, you'll find tiny curly red Noodle-hairs turning up in the weirdest places. It's mysterious. But she leaves a trace behind. It's like that with my mom—and with your Abuelo. When someone we love leaves us—if they die or move away—their love lingers. It leaves a trace behind."

"Like curly red Noodles," Gabriel said.

"Exactly like that," Andrea said.

"This all *sounds* nice," he said. "But I don't believe it. I won't see my abuelo again. Not as a person. Not as a noodle. Not as an anything. He's gone and I hate it."

The tension rose in the room. If I know one thing about people feeling tense, it's that a good walk always helps. Plus, I had to pee. So I stood up and brought Gabriel my leash.

Andrea smiled.

"What would you think about taking Noodle for a little walk?" Andrea said. "I have an idea."

CHAPTER 7

Gabriel and I led the way back to campus. He walked fast so I kicked into a trot. My hair flopped around my vest.

"*Que linda,*" Abuela said. "Noodle is a good girl. Reminds me of my Pepe back in México."

"Mama," Isabel said. "You said Pepe was out-of-control."

"Well, yes," Abuela. "He was wild, but he was beautiful. I still remember when your abuelo brought Pepe home. Abuelo found him at the rail yards. Your abuelo loved to rescue animals and people."

"See?" Andrea said. "That memory is like a

'noodle' from your abuelo."

Gabriel gripped my leash tighter and bent down to pat my head.

"Great," Gabriel said. "I'll just visit Noodle instead of going to the cemetery."

"What if Noodle came with you to the cemetery?" Andrea asked. "She's used to visiting graves and memorial sites."

"Could she do that?" Gabriel asked. We both slowed to a regular walk. I was eager to get my trot back, but it was up to Gabriel. "I mean, if I have to go to the dumb cemetery, I'd rather go with Noodle."

"If it's okay with your mom and abuela," Andrea said. "Noodle would be happy to go."

"Is it?" Gabriel asked. He stopped walking and turned back to his mom.

"Of course," Gabriel's mom said. "Noodle is welcome."

"Wonderful," Andrea said. "But first, Noodle

wants to show you something."

We crossed through the iron gates that led to campus. I got my trot back as we headed over the bridge and turned on the path that wound along the river.

"The tree!" Andrea said.

Dogs understand more words than most people realize. *Treat. Walk. Sit. Stay. Vet. Park.* Those are some of the most common ones. I know all those—and lots more. But two of my favorites are: *The Tree.*

"See this tree?" Andrea said. "It's no ordinary tree. You might call it a 'curly red noodle.'"

"Why?" Gabriel asked.

"Well," Andrea said. "The students missed Mr. Fusilli so much, they raised money and planted this tree. To remember him! They were sad he was gone, but wanted a reminder to show everyone how nice he was.

I squatted next to the tree to give Mr. Fusilli

my usual greeting and sniffed to see if that possum had been back.

Gabriel giggled. "That's not a nice way to remember someone, Noodle!" he said.

"But that's how dogs let other animals know they've been around," Andrea said. "Sometimes I think she does it to let Mr. Fusilli know she remembers him too."

"So Noodle wasn't mad after Mr. Fusilli died?" Gabriel asked.

"Oh, she was sad. She cried a lot—and didn't eat well for a couple weeks," Andrea said. "That may have been because she was mad. But with time and a lot of walks and snuggles, she got better. I'm sure she still misses him. But she found joy again. I want to show you one more thing: see that plaque?"

Andrea pointed to a metal rectangle in the dirt.

Gabriel moved over to read it.

"*To Antoni Fusilli. A man who loved his dog and the students at this college. He listened to our worries, told us stories, and changed our lives. His legacy lives on forever,*" Gabriel read.

"What does that mean?" Gabriel asked.

"A legacy is like a red noodle left in your apartment," Andrea said. "It's a sign you were there—and that you made the world a better place. What's your abuelo's legacy? What signs did he leave you?"

Gabriel looked at the buildings and took a

deep breath.

"He, he, he…." Gabriel began to cry.

Gabriel squatted down next to me and wiped his face in my hair. I leaned into him and let him sob against me. It was good to smell the tears finally falling down his face.

"He made me better," Gabriel finally said.

I slurped and slurped the tears off his face. He put his arms around my neck.

But then, something hit my nose. A smell. I looked to The Tree to see if it came from the ground.

Lemon. Honey.

No, not from there.

I put my nose into the air and sniffed. Gabriel wiped his face and looked at me.

"What is it?" He asked.

Lemon. Honey. Mixed with something else that was so familiar.

Then I heard a cough.

I looked up. I stood up. My tail wagged and wagged.

I barked and barked and barked.

I pulled at the end of my leash and broke free from Gabriel's loose grip.

"Noodle!" Andrea called after me.

But I couldn't stop.

He looked like a man now. But I would know him anywhere. That was Jimmy.

That was my boy Jimmy.

CHAPTER 8

Jimmy stopped as I ran toward him. He bent down to greet me.

"I used to have a dog just like you," he said. "You look just like my Curly."

"Really?" said Nate, who was standing next to Jimmy. "Because her name is Curly Noodle."

Jimmy froze. He held my head in his hands.

"Is it you? Is it really you?" He said.

I licked him and licked him and leapt and crawled all over him. We wrestled in the grass like old times. Jimmy laughed and coughed.

"I am *so sorry!*" Andrea said. She ran to catch up. "Noodle, sit!"

I sat. But my butt shook and wiggled.

"She knows better than to act like this with her vest on," Andrea said.

"It's okay," Jimmy said as he stood up to greet everyone.

"It's really *not* okay," Andrea said. She breathed in and out. "She's a Helper Hound. She should not…"

"Andrea," Nate said. "This is Jimmy. Noodle's *first* boy."

"You're the one with allergies?" Gabriel asked.

Jimmy laughed. "Yes, well," he said. "How did you know?"

"Long story," Andrea said. "I can't believe you're here. Are you visiting North Branch?"

"I am," Jimmy said. "Nate is giving me a tour of the campus. But what is Curly doing here?

"She's my dog," Andrea said. "We live here."

Jimmy took a deep breath and hugged me. I jumped and jumped and slurped and slurped.

"I can't believe this," he said. Jimmy sat on the ground. I sat on him.

"I was so mad at Mom after you left," Jimmy said. "I didn't talk to her for a week! Then, I'd find your silly red hairs in the craziest places. I'd get so sad. Every night I'd pray that some day I'd see you again. I rode my bike to the shelter one day. They said an older man adopted you—and that he lived near North Branch. That's how I first learned about the school. I've wanted to go to college here since I was 12!"

Andrea laughed and wiped the tears that streamed down her face.

"This is a miracle," Abuela said. "A sign."

Gabriel nodded slowly and reached down to pet me.

"So," Jimmy asked, "Are you her boy now?"

Gabriel shook his head.

"I just met Noodle today. My grandpa died and she's helping me."

Jimmy shook his head.

"I'm sorry, man," he said. "My grandpa died last year. Stinks. I still miss him."

"Me too," Gabriel said. "Do you ever feel mad?"

"Sometimes," Jimmy said. "Like, I'm mad I can't tell him about looking at college. But more sad than mad. You know? My grandpa would go nuts about this story. He'd be so happy to know I found Curly—err—Noodle."

"My abuelo loved to rescue people and animals," Gabriel said. "And he loved when family was together. He'd love this story too."

"I bet Mr. Fusilli, your abuelo, and my grandpa are together somewhere watching us," Jimmy said. "They're probably laughing and …"

"… and smoking cigars," Gabriel said.

Jimmy laughed.

"My grandpa smoked a cigar too!" Jimmy said. "It's terrible. Turns out, *THAT* was what I

was allergic too. Not Noodle! Never smoke, kid,
okay?"

Gabriel nodded and sat down next to me.

Thunder rumbled in the distance. We all
looked up to the sky. Dark clouds blew across it.

"Looks like a storm," Isabel said.

"Or Abuelo's cigar smoke…" Gabriel said
with a smile. Jimmy laughed.

"See?" Andrea said. "Signs of your abuelo are everywhere."

Abuela shook her head but then winked at Andrea. Then she blew a kiss into the sky.

Andrea suggested we all get lemonade and cookies at our house. The storm came fast. We ran through the rain and burst into the house. I shook all the water off of me—and onto everyone else.

It was okay. Everyone laughed.

Andrea got everyone towels and told the story of how I became a Helper Hound. Abuela and Isabel talked about Pepe and life in Mexico with Abuelo. Gabriel laughed so hard lemonade came out of nose. Then everyone laughed harder. I licked the crumbs off the floor.

This was the best day.

Before Jimmy left to catch a train home, he asked Gabriel to do him a favor.

"Sure," Gabriel said.

"Curly Noodle has helped lots of people in her life," Jimmy said. "She helped me, she helped Mr. Fusilli, she helped you, and she helped all those people we just heard about. Noodle makes us all better. That's her legacy."

Gabriel nodded.

"So, could you do me a favor?" Jimmy asked Gabriel. "You think you can help *her*?"

"Yeah!" Jimmy said. "But what does she need?"

Jimmy bent down to whisper. "Noodle's got a great life here. I see that. But she loved playing with me when I was a kid. I bet she misses that. Would you be her boy? Would you stop by and play with her some days? Andrea and your mom said it would be okay."

Gabriel knelt down beside me.

"You want me to come play?" he asked.

I slurped his face. I did. I really did.

Jimmy turned toward the door. He had a

train to catch. But he'd come back to visit.

"You know, last time I didn't get to say goodbye to Noodle," Jimmy said. "It's nice to say goodbye to her now. Can't wait to see you again, Curly."

My tail wagged and wagged as Jimmy walked out the door. He'd be back. I knew it.

"I never really got to say goodbye to Abuelo," Gabriel said.

"No, niño," Abuela said. "He died before we could."

"When Noodle comes with us to the cemetery, I can say goodbye to Abuelo there," Gabriel said. "But I can also tell him about Jimmy and Noodle. And, that I know now that I will see him again."

EPILOGUE

Dear Noodle:

Thanks for coming with me to help me say goodbye to Abuelo. I'm still sad, but Andrea was right. I don't feel so mad any more. It's weird! I just keep smiling. It's fun imagining Abuelo, Mr. Fusilli, and Jimmy's grandpa together. It's cool that we all know each other now. It helps.

Abuela is going to walk me over to your house when you get back from your "refresher" course. Mom said you had to go back to Helper Hounds University because you ran across to Jimmy. I know you were not supposed to, but I don't blame you. I'd run if I saw my abuelo!

Anyway, we can play when you get back. I got you a new rope toy. We can try that out. Plus, I'll throw you my old baseball. I need to work on my pitching. Abuelo used to help me with that. But now I have you!

Mom said Jimmy is starting college at North Branch this fall. That means we get to play with him all the time! That'll be fun. Though, Mom said he'll be in college and more interested in friends his own age and girls... So I need to give him space. Good thing you have a big backyard! Room enough for all of us.

Oh, tell Andrea that I found another one of your red noodles on our floor. I reminded me of you and my abuelo.

Anyway, I should go now. Mom needs help putting away the groceries.

Your friend—

Gabriel

Noodle's
Tips for Grieving

Losing someone you love is really hard. There's no way around that. But I've learned a few things that help.

TIP #1: Bark—I mean, talk—about it! When Mr. Fusilli died, I barked and barked and cried and cried. This helps to get help—but also to get our feelings out. It's okay to talk about how sad you feel. And it's okay to cry or even get angry.

TIP #2: Go places that help you remember your loved one. Some people like to visit grave sites. Some people like to snuggle on their bed. Other people like to walk by a house or go to a favorite restaurant or other favorite place. This can help us relive happy memories or good stories.

TIP #3: Write letters. Dogs can't do this—but people can! Keep a journal or write letters to the people (or pets!) you miss. What do you wish you could tell them? Write that down! This makes loved ones feel close by.

TIP #4: Sense the "Noodles" around you. Noodles are things that remind us of our loved ones. Sometimes noodles are objects, but other times they are smells or sounds! Any time you see or taste or smell or hear something that sparks a memory of your loved one, remember: they aren't so far away and you can "see" them again.

TIP #5: Be thankful. We feel sad when people or dogs die because we loved them. So, we can give thanks for having people or pets to love. We can be thankful for the good times and for all we learned. Death is sad. But love is the best—and it never dies!

FUN FACTS
About Goldendoodles

You've probably heard of lots of dog breeds, such as German Shepherds, or Chihuahuas, or Dachshunds. But have you ever heard of a Goldendoodle? That is a funny name for a very interesting kind of dog.

A Goldendoodle is not an actual dog breed the way a German Shepherd is. Instead, it is a cross-breed, or hybrid breed. That means it is the result of breeding two dogs that are different breeds. In this case, a Goldendoodle is what happens when a Golden Retreiver and a Poodle have puppies.

Goldendoodles, like other cross-breeds, are sometimes called "designer dogs." That's because these dogs do not occur naturally. Instead, people breed different dogs to create, or design this type of animal. Goldendoodles first appeared in the early 1990s and got their name in 1992.

However they come about, Goldendoodles are more than just a funny name. These dogs combine the best of both breeds. Like Poodles, they are very smart. Like Golden Retrievers, they love to play and are very friendly toward both people and other dogs. Although these dogs can get pretty big, weighing up to 100 pounds, they are usually easy to train and make great companions.

Most of all, Goldendoodles love to play! These dogs are great at agility work, where they can show off by running and jumping over obstacles on a course. Many also enjoy swimming. And long walks with their human friends are a Goldendoodle's idea of a great day.

Many Goldendoodles work as service dogs or therapy dogs. Because these dogs don't bark as much as other dogs and also don't shed as much, they are good companions for people who might not be able to be around other dog breeds. Most of all, the Goldendoodle's friendly, playful personality makes it a great friend for people of all ages.